WHY KINGS AND QUEENS DON'T WEAR CROWNS

Published by
Skandisk, Inc.
6667 West Old Shakopee Road, Suite 109
Bloomington, Minnesota 55438
www.skandisk.com

Originally published as
Hvorfor de kongelige ikke har krone på hodet,
Copyright © 2004 J.W. Cappelens Forlag, AS, Oslo

First English Edition copyright © 2005 Skandisk, Inc.
Second Printing 2005
Text copyright © 2004 by Princess Märtha Louise
Illustrations copyright © 2004 by Svein Nyhus
Translated by Mari Elise Sevig-Fajardo

Interior design and typesetting by
Koechel Peterson and Associates, Inc., Mpls, MN.

ISBN 10: 1-57534-037-2
ISBN 13: 978-1-57534-037-1

Library of Congress Control Number: 2005924449

Printed in Mexico
12 11 10 09 08 07 06 05   2 3 4 5

Why Kings and Queens Don't Wear Crowns

A Fairy Tale By
Princess
Märtha Louise

With Illustrations By
SVEIN NYHUS

Translated By
MARI ELISE SEVIG-FAJARDO

SKANDISK INC.

Once upon a time there was a little prince on his way from Denmark to Norway for the first time with his father and mother, King Haakon and Queen Maud. The year was 1905, and they had been chosen to become the new Norwegian royal family. The waves were rough and the little prince was cold and afraid. The little prince's name was actually Alexander Edward Christian Frederick, but the king thought that name was too long and too Danish, now that he was going to be the prince of Norway. So they decided to call him Olav, because that was an old Norwegian royal name.

When King Haakon stepped off the boat in Kristiania, the city we call Oslo today, his was the first Norwegian royal foot to touch Norwegian soil for several hundred years. Many people at the harbor were shouting, "Long live the king!" They waved Norwegian flags, just as they do on Norway's Constitution Day, May 17th. But this was the 25th of November. All the noise scared little Olav. He was only two years old and didn't understand what this commotion was all about. But one thing he did understand. Now he was going to get a crown, just like his great-grandparents, the king and queen of Denmark. Back then, kings and queens didn't do much besides sit on their thrones and make decisions for their country, of course. Olav thought that sounded like fun. He couldn't wait to sit on a throne with a crown on his head!

Every time little Olav saw a painting of a man or a woman wearing a crown, he pointed and said, "Crown, crown!" And the royal attendants who always followed him around smiled and said, "Yes, that's right. That's a crown. And soon Your Royal Highness will get one, too." Little Olav wondered who "Your Royal Highness" was.

As the months went by, little Olav became impatient. Where were the crowns? But then one day all the grown-ups started talking about a coronation. Little Olav wondered what that was all about. "Crown?" he asked the queen one day, and she explained that now they were going to Trondheim to get crowned in the Nidaros Cathedral. Little Olav jumped for joy. Finally, he would have a crown and get to sit on a throne!

The day arrived and the city of Trondheim sizzled with excitement. Even the sun came out to warm the day and smile upon King Haakon, Queen Maud, and Prince Olav. The Nidaros Cathedral was decorated royally for the occasion. Norwegian flags streamed from every post and pillar. Little Olav watched excitedly as the king and queen were crowned. Finally, it was his turn. Little Olav's crown was the smallest because he was the smallest. It was made of shiny gold and precious jewels. The women of the royal court applauded and exclaimed, "Oh, my! What a gorgeous crown Your Royal Highness is wearing!" and little Olav beamed as brightly and proudly as his crown. *It wasn't their fault that they didn't know his name was Olav,* he thought.

When the royal family came home again to the palace in Kristiania, there were three thrones set up in the biggest hall. Little Olav got the smallest one because he was the smallest. They sat on their thrones with the crowns on their heads, wearing their finest royal robes. What a sight to behold!

After a few weeks, little Olav thought sitting on the throne was extremely boring. It didn't help that people saw him and exclaimed, "Oh, my! What a lovely crown Your Royal Highness is wearing!"

Summer turned to winter, and little Olav, who'd grown so tired of sitting on his throne wearing his crown, screamed whenever he had to sit there. He cried night and day. He made such a fuss that the king and queen decided to send him outside to learn more about Norway instead of sitting on his throne all day. After all, they were from Denmark, and everything in Norway was new to them. He was very excited and promised to be very, very careful with his crown.

A nanny accompanied little Olav on his royal mission because the king and queen had to sit on their thrones wearing their crowns. They couldn't possibly watch him at the same time!

One day, as little Olav and his nanny strolled through the park by the palace, they came upon some children making a snowman.

"Who are you? And where did you get that crown?" asked the children.

"I am the prince who lives in the palace," said little Olav, "and I am trying to learn about Norwegian customs and traditions."

"Look no further!" said the children, "because making snowmen is something very Norwegian."

"Now, be careful with your crown," warned the nanny.

But little Olav didn't listen. He began making snowmen, crowns and all; and the snowmen he made were the finest anyone had ever seen. But when he was done, the nanny discovered a scratch on his crown. What would his parents say?

When he came inside, the king and queen noticed the scratch right away and made him sit on his throne with his crown for three days as punishment. After the three days had passed, little Olav continued on his mission, learning more about Norwegian customs and traditions, because the king and queen still didn't feel they knew enough about the Norwegian people and how they lived.

"We want to be more Norwegian than the Norwegians, even with these crowns on our heads," said the king.

The next day, when little Olav and his nanny were out in the park by the palace, they met some children who were sledding.

"Who are you? And where did you get that crown?" asked the children.

"I am the prince who lives in the palace," said little Olav, "and I am trying to learn about Norwegian customs and traditions."

"Look no further!" said the children, "because sledding is something very Norwegian."

"Now, be careful with your crown," warned the nanny.

But little Olav didn't listen. He sat down on the biggest sled and raced down the hill as fast as lightning! On their way back to the palace, the nanny noticed with horror that a jewel was missing from little Olav's crown. What would his parents say about that? As you might expect, the king and queen were quite upset and made him sit on his throne with his crown for three weeks.

When the three weeks had passed, little Olav was sent out for the third time to learn more about Norwegian customs and traditions. But this time the king and the queen came along to make sure that everything went as it should. "We want to be more Norwegian than the Norwegians, even with these crowns on our heads!" said the king.

He motioned the nanny over to his side and asked her if there might be something his whole family could do together that was very Norwegian.

"Well, Your Majesty, Norwegians are born with skis on their feet," said the nanny shyly.

"With what on their feet? Explain yourself. I don't understand what you mean!"

"Skis, Your Majesty. They look like wooden boards with a pointed tip. You will not be considered a real Norwegian until you master the art of skiing."

"Fetch these wooden boards you speak of, enough for my whole family," ordered the king. So the best ski makers in the land were hired to make skis for the royal family.

It was a cold, clear winter day, when the king, queen, and little Olav got their first pair of skis. Little Olav got the smallest skis, because he was the smallest. When they had skied a little while, they met some children who were ski jumping.

"Who are you? And where did you get that crown?" the children asked.

"I am the prince who lives in the palace," said little Olav, "and I am trying to learn about Norwegian customs and traditions."

"Look no further," said the children, "because ski jumping is something very Norwegian."

But the moment Olav was about to take off, his nanny caught him and said that if he skied down the hill, he would have to sit on his throne forever, because the crown would be ruined for sure! Instead, she placed his skis between hers and whispered to him that they were going to do something fun that would not damage his crown. They had actually practiced in the palace halls, even with his skis on! He had learned to herringbone in the Conservatory and to stand in downhill position in the Ballroom. She set out down the hill, holding on to little Olav, who shrieked with joy. He sped down the hill, more quickly and skillfully than they had ever seen a prince ski. When they reached the bottom of the hill, Olav's crown was sitting sideways on his head! But the nanny adjusted his crown before they headed up the hill again. The king and queen ordered the nanny to teach them, too.

"Your Majesties must be careful with your crowns," warned the nanny.

"Nonsense," said the king. "If my little prince can ski with his crown on, so can I."

The nanny curtsied deeply and explained how to snowplow, bend at the knees, herringbone, and stop.

The king and queen took off together. The queen screamed, and little Olav couldn't tell whether it was for joy or fear. But her screams could be heard for miles! She had missed the first turn and had fallen under a spruce tree. Her long dress billowed like a balloon behind her. There she lay, skis up in the air and head down in the snow, while snow from the tree drifted down on her. The king hit a tree a little farther down the hillside. With arms and legs tangled in the twigs and branches, and snow falling from above, he called out for help. The royal court rushed to his rescue, but they sank into the deep snow. After skiing just a few feet, they were sprawled out in the snow, skis and poles intertwined.

When the people of the royal court were back on their feet again, the king shouted, "Where's my crown?"

Indeed, where were the crowns? Everyone looked around frantically. There was not a crown in sight, except for little Olav's. A search party was organized.

Hours later, when the royal family was back at the palace, enjoying their third cup of hot cocoa by the fire, they got word that the crowns had been found. The master of the court presented them to the royal couple, but they were a mangled mess! The crowns were crooked, bent out of shape, and missing some precious jewels.

"If I may speak my mind, Your Majesty, I would suggest you not stand on those boards anymore."

"Nonsense," said the king, who felt he was just beginning to understand Norwegian customs and traditions. "If we are going to be more Norwegian than the Norwegians, we have to ski like the Norwegians do! The crowns are the problem! You simply must find a solution."

The master of the court bowed and left the room, shaking his head. *All that fresh air has gone to the king's head,* he thought to himself. He called together a meeting of the royal court, which lasted three days.

At the end of the third day, the master of the court came back triumphantly. He was bursting with pride because he had found a great glorious solution to present to the king, the queen, and the little prince.

"Your Majesties, Your Royal Highness," he began. "The royal attendants suggest that the crowns be taken to Trondheim, where they can be put on display, if the king allows. Then Your Majesties and the prince can become as Norwegian as you like, without putting your precious crowns in danger."

The king thought this was such a brilliant idea that he clapped his hands.

But poor little Olav was disappointed. He didn't want to part with his crown. The queen bent down and explained, "You see, my little one, the crown you are wearing on your head is only for decoration. The crown that matters most is the one you wear in your heart."

From that day on, the royal family wore their crowns in their hearts and not on their heads. The crowns were driven to Trondheim, where they can be seen to this day, and they are taken out and worn only on very special occasions.

King Haakon, Queen Maud, and Prince Olav became excellent skiers. And when Olav grew up, he even jumped at Holmenkollen, the most famous ski jump in Norway, with a personal record of 33 meters. So, it's a good thing he didn't have to wear a crown on his head! Norwegians came to love and respect their new royal family, who worked so hard to be truly Norwegian, and they all skied happily ever after.